Hurray for Barbara Park and the Junie B. Jones books!

"Park, one of the funniest writers around…brings her refreshing humor to the beginning chapter-book set." —*Booklist*

"Park convinces beginning readers that Junie B.— *and* reading—are lots of fun." —*Publishers Weekly*

"Park is simply hilarious." —America Online's *The Book Report*

"The honesty and inventiveness of this savvy kindergartner make the Junie B. books accessible and completely enjoyable." —*School Library Journal*

"Park has a wonderful ear for the dialogue of five-year-olds and an even better grasp of how their minds operate." —*Booklist*

"Junie B. Jones is a likable character whose comic mishaps…will elicit laughs from young readers." —*The Horn Book*

"A genuinely funny, easily read story." —*Kirkus Reviews*

The Junie B. Jones series

Junie B. Jones
Has a
Peep in Her Pocket

by Barbara Park
illustrated by Denise Brunkus

SCHOLASTIC INC.

New York   Toronto   London   Auckland   Sydney
Mexico City   New Delhi   Hong Kong

ISBN 0-439-22309-1

Text copyright © 2000 by Barbara Park.
Illustration copyright © 2000 by Denise Brunkus.
All rights reserved.
Published by Scholastic Inc., 555 Broadway, New York, NY 10012,
by arrangement with Random House Children's Books,
a division of Random House, Inc.
SCHOLASTIC and associated logos are trademarks
and/or registered trademarks of Scholastic Inc.

12 11   2 3 4 5/0

Printed in the U.S.A.   40

First Scholastic printing, September 2000

Contents

1/ Confusing Stuff

My name is Junie B. Jones. The B stands for Beatrice. Except I don't like Beatrice. I just like B and that's all.

I am almost six years old.

Almost six is when you get to go to school. And so, last summer Mother took me to the school office. And she 'rolled me in afternoon kindergarten.

'Rolled is the grown-up word for *signed me up and made me go.*

Only guess what?

I don't even mind going there, hardly. 'Cause I made two bestest friends at that place, that's why!

Their names are Lucille and that Grace.

We are like three peas in a row.

My teacher's name is Mrs. She has another name, too. But I just like Mrs. and that's all.

Only here is the trouble. Just when I was getting good at kindergarten, Mrs. made a 'nouncement to our class. And she said that pretty soon, school is going to end!

I did a gasp at that terrible news.

"No, Mrs.! No, no, no! How can school *end*? 'Cause Mother said I have to go to school till I am an old teenager. And I am not even six years old yet!"

Mrs. quick shaked her head.

"Oh dear, I'm sorry, Junie B.," she said.

"I'm afraid that you've misunderstood me. School isn't going to end *forever*. School will just be taking a summer vacation."

She smiled at me. "You, and everyone else in this class, will come back to school in September. It's just that you won't be in Room Nine anymore."

I quick got out a paper and crayon.

"Okey-doke. Then tell me the name of our new room," I said. "'Cause I will need to tell Mother where to bring me."

Mrs. did a little frown. "I'm sorry," she said again. "But right now, I have no idea what room you'll be in next year."

Now I did a frown, too.

"So what am I s'posed to do, then? Just wander around the school until I find you people?"

Mrs. looked funny at me.

"You still don't understand," she said. "Next year you're going to have a *different* teacher, Junie B. Next year you're going to be in *first*."

"First what?" I asked.

"First *grade,*" she said.

Just then, my stomach felt sickish inside. 'Cause I don't even *like* first graders, that's why. First graders are bullies to me at recess.

And I don't want to be in the same room as those guys.

Pretty soon, a boy named William started to sniffle very much. 'Cause William hates first graders even more than me.

That's because one time a first grader stoled William's winter hat with the ear flaps. And he put it on a dog that was running around the playground. And the dog runned away with William's ear-flap hat forever.

I patted William very nice.

"Me and William don't want to be in the same room as first graders," I told Mrs. "Me and William prefer children our own age."

"Me too," said my bestest friend Lucille. "I prefer children my own age, too."

"Me too," hollered a boy named Paulie Allen Puffer.

"Me too," said a girl named Charlotte.

Mrs. said *shh* to us.

"Boys and girls, *please*. Now everyone is misunderstanding me," she said. "We need to get clear on this right now. Next year— when you come back to school—you will *not* be in class with the children who are first graders this year. Next year, those children will move up to *second* grade. And *you* people will move to first. Understand?"

I thought and thought about that.

Then, all of a sudden, a light bulb came on in my head.

"Ohhh! I get it now! *All* of the grades move up! Right, Mrs.? Everyone does!"

She clapped her hands. "Right! Exactly!" she said very happy. "Now may I please get on with my announcement?"

I brushed my skirt very smoothie.

"Yes, you may," I said real polite.

"Okay," said Mrs. "As I started to tell you earlier, I have very happy news for Room Nine. Because this year—for the first time ever—we are going to go on a special end-of-the-year field trip!"

She smiled real big. "We're going to a farm! Doesn't that sound like fun?"

"A FARM!" shouted the children. "A FARM! A FARM! WE'RE GOING TO A FARM!"

Then Lucille hugged me very thrilled.

"A farm!" she said real squealy in my ear.

"A farm," I said real glum.

'Cause guess what?

Farms are not my favorites.

2 / **Stubby**

That night, I ate dinner with Mother and Daddy and my baby brother named Ollie.

Only I couldn't even swallow that good. 'Cause I was still upset about the field trip, that's why.

"I don't want to go," I said. "I don't want to go to the farm with Room Nine. 'Cause a farm is the most dangerous place I ever heard of."

Daddy looked surprised at me.

"What are you talking about, Junie B.?"

he said. "What's dangerous about a farm?"

"The ponies, of course," I said. "The ponies are dangerous. Farms have ponies running in their fields. And ponies can stomple you into the ground and kill you to death."

Mother covered her face with her hands.

"No, Junie B., *please*. Not this pony thing again. We've talked about this a hundred times. I've told you over and over that ponies do not hurt you."

"Yes, they do too hurt you, Mother!" I said. "I saw it on TV with my own eyeballs!"

Mother looked at Daddy.

"It was that stupid cable show the babysitter let her watch," she said. "It was called—"

"*WHEN PONIES ATTACK*," I

hollered. "IT WAS CALLED *WHEN PONIES ATTACK!*"

After that, Daddy covered his face, too. Then, all of a sudden, he busted out in a loud hoot of laughing. And he couldn't even stop himself.

Mother's cheeks sucked way into her head.

"Thank you," she said. "You're being a huge help here."

Then Daddy got up from his chair. And he went to his room for a time-out.

That's when me and Mother had another long talk about ponies.

She told me that her uncle Billy used to have a farm. And that the farm had a pony named Stubby. And that Stubby was gentle as a lamb.

"As a matter of fact, Uncle Billy had

almost every kind of farm animal you can think of," said Mother. "Pigs, cows, sheep, chickens, goats. He even had a mean old rooster named Spurs. But out of all those animals, the pony was the sweetest."

Mother smiled. "You would have loved Stubby, Junie B.," she said. "He used to follow me around like a puppy."

"He did?" I said.

"He did," she said back. "Honest, honey. I would *never* let you go to a farm if there was even the teeniest chance you would be hurt by any of the animals. But my uncle Billy's farm had the gentlest animals I ever saw."

Mother smiled a little bit. "Well, except for that mean old rooster, anyway," she said.

Just then, Daddy came back into the kitchen.

He said a 'pology to me.

"I'm sorry, Junie B. I didn't mean to laugh. But that TV show you saw was just so ridiculous, I couldn't help it."

After that, he sat down at the table. And he filled out my permission slip for the farm.

"You're going to love this trip," he told me. "We'll get you one of those little throwaway cameras from the drugstore. And you can take pictures of all the animals you see."

"Great idea," said Mother. "And I'll take you shopping for a brand-new pair of overalls. And I'll even pack you your very favorite lunch."

After that, I got down from my chair very quiet. And I went to my room.

Then I climbed onto my bed. And I hugged my stuffed animals real tight.

'Cause I kept on thinking and thinking about what Mother said about Uncle Billy's animals. But mostly, I kept thinking about that mean old rooster.

On account of one time at my school, a boy named meanie Jim brought his rooster for Pet Day. And he said that roosters can peck your head into a nub. And that is not pleasant, I tell you.

I hugged my animals even tighter.

'Cause guess what?

Roosters are a jillion times scarier than ponies.

3/ Pictures

The next morning, Mother called me for breakfast.

"Good morning," said Mother.

"Good morning," said Daddy.

"Good morning," I said. "Roosters can peck your head into a nub."

Daddy put down his coffee cup. "Excuse me?"

I pointed to my head.

"A nub," I explained. "A nub is a teensy

little knob head. Roosters can peck your head into one."

Mother looked strange at me. "What in the world is *this* about?"

I did a big breath at her.

'Cause how can I even be clearer on this subject?

"A nub! A nub! A roundish, ballish head knob! And do not tell me that roosters do not peck you. On account of we had Pet Day at my school. And meanie Jim brought a rooster to Room Nine. And that boy is a rooster expert."

I looked at her. "Plus also, you said Uncle Billy's rooster was mean, too. Right, Mother? Remember that?"

Mother looked fusstrated at me. Then she put her head on the table. And she

didn't come up for a real long time.

    Finally, she peeked her eyes at Daddy.

    "Now what?" she asked kind of quiet.

    "Maybe it'll blow over," said Daddy.

    I shook my head.

    "No, it will *not* blow over," I told them.

"'Cause roosters do not listen to reason. And so there is nothing we can do about this pecking situation."

Daddy rubbed his eyes. "Could we please just change the subject?" he said.

"Yeah, only not talking about a nub will not make it go away," I said. "And so—"

"That's *enough*," said Daddy very growly.

I quick stopped talking then.

But even after we changed the subject, nubs kept staying on my mind.

That day at school, Mrs. told us to draw a picture about our trip to the farm. She said to make it a colorful picture of what we wanted to see there.

I drawed and drawed. Plus also, I colored and colored.

19

When all of us got done with our pictures, we sat our chairs in a big circle. And
we told each other about what we drew.

My bestest friend named Lucille went
first.

She drawed a picture of a pink flamingo.

"Flamingos are my favorite animals,"
she said. "That's because pink is my favorite
color. And flamingos are pink. And I have a
pink dress that will match them perfectly. So
that is the dress I'll be wearing on the field
trip."

She wrinkled her nose real cute.

"Pink brings out the natural blush of my
complexion," she told Mrs. "Have you ever
noticed my satiny-smooth skin?"

Mrs. looked and looked at that girl.

"You're a fascinating child, Lucille. But

I'm afraid there aren't any flamingos on a dairy farm," she said.

Lucille looked surprised.

"So where are they, then?" she asked.

"Well, flamingos can be found a lot of places," said Mrs. "South America, for example."

Lucille shrugged her shoulders. "So, fine. We'll just go there, instead."

Mrs. said for Lucille to please sit down.

Just then, Paulie Allen Puffer sprang out of his chair.

"Look, Teacher! I drew a catfish!" he said. "See his whiskers? My brother said catfish whiskers are so sharp they can slice your finger to the bone."

Mrs. made a sick face.

"Yes, well, thank you for sharing that,

Paulie Allen. But we're not going fishing. We're going to a *farm*, remember?"

Paulie Allen Puffer looked upset.

"Yes, but my brother said there's *lots* of catfish farms around here. And so that's the kind of farm I think we should—"

"*No*, Paulie. No," said Mrs. "We're just going to a regular, plain old farm. With regular, plain old farm animals."

Paulie Allen Puffer did a mad breath.

He said the word *big whoop*.

After that, Paulie Allen Puffer had to stand in the hall.

Mrs. did some deep breathing.

"Please, children. Please. Did *anyone* in Room Nine draw a picture of a regular farm animal? Anyone at all. That's all I'm looking for here. Just a regular old farm animal."

"I did! I did, Mrs.!" I yelled real excited. "I drew a picture of a rooster under a tree!"

"Oh, Junie B.! Thank you! That's perfect!" she said.

I held it up so she could see it.

"See it, Mrs.? See how pretty it is?"

Mrs. looked at my picture.

"Oh yes. That's a *very* nice tree, Junie B.," she said. "But why is it lying on its side?"

"It crashed over in a rainstorm," I said.

"Oh," said Mrs. "Oh dear."

She looked even closer.

"But I'm afraid I don't see the rooster, honey."

I pointed.

"There," I said. "See his foot under the branch? He did not get out in time, apparently."

Mrs. covered her mouth with her hand.

Just then, a girl named Charlotte

hollered, "I hate that picture! That's a terrible picture!"

I crossed my arms at that girl.

"You would not say that if your head was a nub, sister," I said.

Meanie Jim laughed real loud.

Then Mrs. said for all of us to take our chairs back to our tables.

And we did not show any more farm pictures.

4/ Cockle-Doodly-Doo

On Saturday, Mother came into my room. She said we were going shopping for clothes for the farm trip.

I looked up from my coloring book.

"No thank you," I said. "On account of I am getting a fever that day. So I won't actually be going to the farm."

Mother laughed. "Don't be silly," she said.

Then she picked me up. And she carried me out to the car.

"Yeah, only here's the problem. You are not respecting my wishes," I said.

Mother laughed some more. "I promise. This will be fun."

I did a huffy breath. "Whatever," I said.

Whatever is the grown-up word for *that is the dumbest thing I ever heard.*

And guess what?

I was right. Shopping was not fun at all. 'Cause Mother kept on making me try on clothes that I didn't want.

First she made me try on a shirt with checkery squares. Then she made me try on overalls with big, giant pockets. Plus she tied a bandanna around my neck. And she put a straw hat on my head.

I looked in the mirror at myself.

"What do you know…I'm a cornball," I said.

Only too bad for me. 'Cause Mother said
I looked cute as a button. And she bought
those clothes anyway. Plus also, she bought

me a throw-away camera at the drugstore.

After we got home, I started to color again.

Mother hanged up my new clothes.

"Do you want me to show you how to use the camera for your trip now?" she asked.

"No thank you," I said. "On account of I am getting a fever that day. So I won't actually be going to the farm."

After that, Mother did a big sigh.

And she closed my door.

And she let me color in peace.

I got tricked!

'Cause on the day of the trip, I told Mother I had a fever. But that woman did not even take my word for it.

Instead, she took my temperature!

And so what kind of trust is that, I ask you?

"No fever," she said.

Then Mother dressed me in my farm clothes. And she drove me right to my school.

We pulled into the parking lot.

"Oh no!" I said. "Oh no! Oh no!"

'Cause the bus was there for the field trip already! It was parked right at the curb!

"Believe me, Junie B.," said Mother. "You are going to have a great day."

Then she got me out of the car. And she pulled me to my teacher.

"Good morning, Junie B.," said Mrs. "Don't you look cute today?"

I felt my forehead.

"I'm ill," I said.

Mrs. smiled. "I love your straw hat."

"My head is a flaming fireball," I said.

Mrs. bended down next to me. "And that bandanna is absolutely darling."

"I am burning to a crinkle," I told her.

"*Crisp*," said Mother.

"Whatever," I said.

After that, Mother lifted me onto the bus. And she handed me my backpack with my lunch and camera.

She waved good-bye to me.

I did not wave back. 'Cause my hand did not feel friendly.

Just then, my bestest friend named Grace came running to get me.

"Junie B.! Junie B.! Lucille and I saved you a seat!"

Then she grabbed my arm. And she took me way in the back.

I sat down next to Lucille.

"No!" said that Grace. "That's *my* seat, Junie B.!"

She quick pulled me up.

"So where am *I* supposed to sit, then?" I asked.

Lucille pointed across the aisle.

"Right there, silly," she said. "You're sitting right directly across from Grace and me. And so it's almost like we're sitting together. Except you will be separate."

I sat down.

"But there's nobody to talk to over here," I told her.

Just then, that meanie Jim jumped up from the seat behind me.

"Me! You can talk to me!" he said very laughing.

Then he leaned into my ear. And he hollered, "COCKLE-DOODLY-DOO!"

right into my eardrum.

"Too bad you're afraid of roosters," he said. "Roosters can tell if you're afraid, Junie B. Ask anybody. Roosters always peck the scaredy-heads first."

"No, they do not, Jim!" I said back. "You are just making that up, probably. And anyhow, if roosters pecked people's heads off, all farmers would have nub heads. Only they don't. So there. Ha ha."

Jim raised up one eyebrow.

"Are you *sure* all farmers don't have nub heads?" he said kind of spooky. "Hmm? Are you?"

He did a grin. "Why do you think farmers wear *hats*?"

Jim leaned closer. "To cover up their nubs, that's why," he whispered.

After that, he lifted up my hat.

And he patted my head.

And he cockle-doodly-dooed all over again.

5/ E-I-E-I-O

The bus drove for a very long time.

Paulie Allen Puffer was sitting with that Jim I hate. While we were riding, he stood up behind me.

"Junie B.! Junie B.! Listen to the song we just made up!" he said.

Then he and Jim started singing their song as loud as they could:

"Old MacDonald had a nub.

E-I-E-I-O.

And on his nub he had a hat.

E-I-E-I-O.
With an *ow! ow!* here
And an *ow! ow!* there.
Here an *ow!* There an *ow!*
Everywhere an *ow! ow!*
Old MacDonald had a nub.
E-I-E-I-O!"

Finally, I covered my ears with my hands so I couldn't hear them anymore.

Then I singed a loud song of my own.

It is called *"Ha Ha. I Can't Hear You!"*

I invented the words myself.

"Ha ha. I can't hear you!
Ha ha. I can't hear you!
Ha ha. I can't hear you!"

I singed that song a jillion times, I think.

Then, all of a sudden, the bus turned down a long dirt road.

And oh no!

It was the *farm!*

"We're here! We're here! We're here!" shouted the children very thrilled.

I looked out the window.

There was a big house with trees all around it. Also, there was a barn and a tractor and some chickens.

I did a big gulp at those peckery things.

'Cause chickens have pointy lips, just like roosters.

I quick scrunched down on the bus floor.

Then I hided under my backpack very sneaky. 'Cause maybe if I kept real quiet, Mrs. wouldn't see me. And I could hide on the bus the whole entire time.

Lucille and that Grace stood up from their seats. I made the *shh!* sign at them.

"Do not tell the teacher I'm here. And I *mean* it," I whispered.

Only too bad for me. Because just then, I heard the worstest noise in the world.

It was the noise of a big, dumb tattletale boy.

"TEACHER! TEACHER! JUNIE B. JONES IS HIDING ON THE FLOOR! I SEE HER! I SEE HER!" shouted that meanie Jim.

"SHH!" I yelled.

But Jim did not shh.

Instead, he jumped right up on the bus seat. And he pointed his finger at me.

"SHE'S TRYING TO HIDE UNDER HER BACKPACK SO YOU WON'T SEE HER. BUT YOU CAN SEE ALMOST ALL OF HER PERFECTLY GOOD!"

He got off the seat and waved to me very teasing.

"Ta-ta," he said. Then he followed Lucille and Grace right off the bus.

After that, my heart got very poundy inside. 'Cause I heard the sound of footprints, that's why.

I scrunched myself tighter.

"Junie B.?"

It was the voice of Mrs.

I didn't answer her.

"Junie B. I *see* you, okay? Your backpack isn't big enough to hide you," she said.

I looked up real slow.

"Hello. How are you today?" I said kind of nervous. "I am fine. Only I'm not actually hiding."

Mrs. crossed her arms.

"Then what are you actually doing?" she asked me.

I did a gulp.

"I'm tidying," I said.

"Tidying what?" asked Mrs.

I thinked fast.

"I'm tidying the floor," I told her.

I quick took off my bandanna. Then I wiped up the floor with it.

"Good news," I said. "It's tidy now."

All of a sudden, I heard a chuckle.

I turned my head and saw some boots.

"Junie B. Jones," said Mrs., "I would like you to meet Farmer Flores. Farmer Flores owns the beautiful farm we're going to be visiting today."

I raised my eyes very slow.

Then—finally—I looked all the way to the top of his head.

That's when my arms got shivers all over them.

'Cause guess what?

Farmer Flores was wearing a hat.

6/ Farmer Flores

Farmer Flores did a nice smile.

"Your teacher tells me that you're not very happy about being here today," he said.

I felt my forehead again.

"I'm ill," I said.

"Yes, well, I've been thinking about how I could make this a better visit for you. And I was wondering if maybe you would like to be my special farm hand today. Do you know what a special farm hand is, Junie B.?"

I shaked my head no.

"Well, for one thing, the special farm hand gets to walk with the farmer in the very front of the line. Would you like that, do you think?"

I did my shoulders up and down.

"I don't know. Maybe," I said.

"And also, the special farm hand gets to be the very first person to sit on the tractor," said Farmer Flores. "Does that sound like fun to you?"

I sighed very big.

"I don't know. Maybe," I said.

"Oh," he said. "But here's the most important job of all. The special farm hand gets to help me keep all the children in order."

Just then, my mouth came all the way open!

"In *order?*" I asked very thrilled. "You mean I get to order the other children around?"

Farmer Flores rubbed his chin. "Well, yes. I suppose you could put it that way," he said.

I quick grabbed my backpack.

"Well, then what are we waiting for, Farmer?" I said.

After that, I runned off the bus speedy fast. And I clapped my hands real loud.

"ALL RIGHT, PEOPLE. GET IN LINE. FARMER FLORES IS GOING TO SHOW US AROUND! AND HE DOESN'T HAVE ALL DAY, FOLKS!"

Pretty soon, Farmer Flores and Mrs. came off the bus, too.

They told the children to please hold

hands like the buddy system.

"YOU HEARD THEM, PEOPLE!" I hollered. "THE BUDDY SYSTEM! WE WILL BE USING THE BUDDY SYSTEM TODAY!"

All of a sudden, Mrs. bended down next to my ear.

"Helping Farmer Flores does not mean being rude, Junie B.," she said. "I want you to be helpful and nice."

"But I *am* being helpful and nice," I said. "'Cause I didn't even tell anyone to shut up yet."

Just then, I skipped to the end of the line and checked on Paulie Allen Puffer and Jim.

"I've got my eye on you two clowns," I said very helpful and nice.

Jim cockle-doodly-dooed at me again.

"Yeah, only too bad for you, Jim," I said.

"'Cause I already looked around this place for roosters. And I didn't even see one of those meanie guys. So, ha!"

After that, I quick skipped back to the front of the line. And me and Farmer led the children to the pasture.

Pasture is the farm word for *big grass and a fence*.

Only wait till you hear this! There were four horses and two ponies in that pasture!

And I did not even run from them!

"ATTENTION, PEOPLE! ATTENTION!" I hollered. "DO NOT BE AFRAID OF THE HORSES AND PONIES. JUST STAND VERY STILL AND THEY WILL NOT ATTACK YOU...PROBABLY."

I thought for a second.

"ALSO, DO NOT FEED THEM CHEESE POPCORN," I said.

I looked at Farmer. "I learned that from the zoo," I said.

After that, Farmer held my hand. And we led the children to the barn.

The barn is where the cows get milked.

All of Room Nine held their noses in that place. 'Cause barns smell like stink and hay.

Farmer Flores told us all about milking cows. He showed us the machines that hook up to the cows. Plus also, we saw big giant cans that hold the milk.

After he got done, he asked if we had questions.

I raised my hand.

"If you breathe stink air into your body, does it make your insides smell like stink air, too?"

Farmer didn't answer me. Only I don't

know why. 'Cause that is a troubling question, I tell you.

After that, he took my hand again. And we took the children to another part of the barn.

There was a black-and-white cow there. Farmer showed us how to milk her with a milking machine.

That is called a *demo cow*, I believe.

After that, Farmer Flores was finished talking about cows.

"Okay, boys and girls. Let's go back outside and visit some of the other animals," he said.

Just then, I got a little nervous inside. On account of what if he was taking us to see the rooster?

I walked outside very careful.

Only good news! Farmer Flores took us right to pigs in a pen. And after that, we saw goats and lambs. And I petted a lamb on her fuzzy head!

And that is not even the bestest part! On account of pretty soon, Mrs. Farmer Flores drove up on a shiny red tractor! And I was the first one to get to sit up there with her!

I quick gave Mrs. my camera.

"Take my picture, please! Take my picture up here on this tractor!"

I smiled real big for her.

Mrs. clicked me.

"That will be a beaut!" I said.

After that, I got down from the tractor. And I took a cow picture. And a pig picture. And a lamb picture!

Plus also, I took pictures of my bestest friends named Lucille and that Grace.

"Excellent pictures, friends!" I said real thrilled. "I can't wait for Mother and Daddy to see them!"

Then I hurried to the big trash can. And I throwed the camera right in there.

"See, Grace? See, Lucille? It is called a

throw-away camera. Mother said that after you take the pictures, you just throw it away and buy a new one. And so what can be easier than that?"

"Wow!" said Grace.

"I know it is wow, Grace," I said. "Plus Mother said the pictures turn out beautifully."

All of a sudden, Mrs. runned over and she took my camera out of the trash.

"Junie B., honey, you can't throw the camera away *before* the pictures are developed," she said.

"Shoot," I said. "Nothing is ever easy, is it?"

After that, Mrs. put down blankets in the grass. 'Cause it was time for a picnic, of course!

Me and Lucille and that Grace sat on a

blanket and opened our lunch bags.

"Yum," I said. "Egg salad."

"Yum," said that Grace. "Tuna salad."

"Yum," said Lucille. "Crab salad on a flaky croissant, with a side order of greens in a light raspberry vinaigrette dressing."

Then all of us ate our lunches very delicious.

7/ Spike

After lunch, it was time to get the children together again.

I clapped my loud hands some more.

"OKAY, PEOPLE. THE FUN IS OVER. GET YOUR BUDDY AND GET IN LINE. ON ACCOUNT OF FARMER FLORES WANTS TO TALK SOME MORE, APPARENTLY."

Farmer did a teensy frown at me.

Then he holded my hand. And we walked across the yard to another fence.

Inside the fence, there was a building and some chickens.

"Okay, everyone," said Farmer Flores. "This is the last stop on the tour today."

He pointed. "Who can tell me what that little building is right there?"

Lucille jumped up and down real happy.

"The gift shop! The gift shop! I've been wondering where that was!" she said real delighted.

Farmer Flores did a chuckle. "Well, that's a good guess. But most farms don't have gift shops."

He looked at the class. "I'll give you a hint," he said. "My wife and I get eggs for our breakfast every morning from that little house there."

Just then, a boy named Roger jumped up and down and all around.

"I KNOW, I KNOW!" he shouted. "IT'S A HENHOUSE!"

Farmer Flores smiled. "Right!" he said. "It's a house where hens lay their eggs."

Farmer Flores opened the gate.

I tugged on his shirt. He bended down next to me.

"Is there a rooster in there, too?" I asked kind of scared.

"Just one," he said. "But there's lots of chickens. Want to go in and say hello?"

I shook my head real fast. Then I runned away from the gate speedy quick.

Paulie Allen Puffer and Jim laughed and pointed.

"Look at Junie B. Jones!" they hollered. "Junie B. Jones is afraid of roosters!"

Farmer Flores made an angry face at those two.

"Hey, hey, hey!" he said. "I'm surprised at you boys. There's nothing wrong with someone being cautious about roosters."

Just then, some of the other children looked kind of scared, too.

"Why?" asked Lucille. "Is the rooster going to peck us?"

Farmer Flores shook his head. "No," he said. "That old rooster in there is a pretty calm fella. But that doesn't mean Junie B. should be laughed at."

He smiled a little bit.

"Why, I've been around farm animals all my life," he said. "But every once in a while, I still come across an animal that I don't get along with."

Farmer laughed. "In fact, we used to have a goat who nipped at me every time I got near him. And for years, I made my wife go in his pen and feed him."

After that, Farmer Flores winked at me. And Mrs. said I could wait outside the gate.

My shoulders relaxed very much.

I sat down on the grass outside the fence.

Only wait till you hear this. Pretty soon, Farmer leaned over the fence where I was sitting. And he was holding a baby yellow chick!

I giggled and giggled at that cute little thing.

"A chick! A baby chick! Can I hold it, Farmer? Please, please, please?" I asked.

Farmer Flores put the baby chick in my hands.

It was fluffery, and softie, and light as feathers.

"Oooooh, I love it, Farmer! I love this baby chick!"

After that, I put the chick in the grass. And on my lap. And in my straw hat. Plus also, I put it in my big, wide pocket.

I peeked at it in there.

"I wish I could take you home with me," I said. "I wish I could take you home to my house. And then you could live with me and my dog Tickle forever and ever. Would you like that? Huh? Would you?"

The baby chick did a peep.

"Hey! You said yes!" I said.

I turned around. "Did you hear that, Farmer? The baby chick said it would like to come home with me!"

Farmer shook his head.

"Oh, I don't know, Junie B.," he said. "I'm not sure you'd really like having Spike grow up at your house."

I did a frown at that man.

"Spike? Who's Spike?" I asked.

Farmer pointed at the baby chick.

"Spike, the chick," he said. "We named that little guy Spike."

I peeked at the chick again.

"Yeah, only Spike is not actually a good name for a fluffery baby chick," I said.

"I know, Junie B.," he said. "But Spike isn't going to be a little chick forever, you know."

"I know," I said back. "'Cause someday Spike will be a big *giant* chick. Right, Farmer? Right? Right?"

Farmer Flores shook his head again.

"Well, not *exactly*," he said.

I looked at him real curious.

"Well, if Spike won't be a big chick, what's Spike going to be?" I asked.

Farmer Flores took Spike back from me.

He held him in his hands. And patted his little softie head.

"Someday, Junie B.," he said, "Spike will be a *rooster*."

8/ Confusion

I had confusion in my head.

'Cause first I hated roosters.

Only then I liked Spike.

Only Spike is going to be a rooster.

And so now what am I supposed to do?

I didn't talk much after that. 'Cause confusion takes a lot of thinking, that's why.

Plus also, I might need counseling, possibly.

Finally, the children finished seeing the

chickens. And they came out through the gate.

Then Farmer Flores held my hand one more time. And he took us to a field with wild flowers in it.

He said we could pick wild flowers for our mothers! 'Cause that would be like a gift from the gift shop, he said.

After all of us had our flowers, Mrs. took our picture with that nice man.

And here is the bestest part of all!

Farmer Flores took off his hat!

AND HIS HEAD WAS NOT A NUB!

I danced all around that guy very thrilled.

"Farmer Flores! Farmer Flores! Your head is not a nub! Your head is not a nub!"

He wrinkled up his eyebrows. "Uh… thank you," he said kind of quiet.

"You're welcome, Farmer!" I said back. "'Cause guess what? Now I don't have to be afraid of roosters anymore!"

I jumped up and down. "Now maybe I can be afraid of goats! Just like you!" I shouted.

After that, Farmer Flores looked at me a real long time.

Then he rolled his eyes way up to the sky.

I looked up there, too.

But I didn't see anything.

**Junie B. has a lot to say
about everything and everybody...**

noises
If loud, screechy noises get inside your head, you have to take an aspirin. I saw that on a TV commercial.
• from *Junie B. Jones and the Stupid Smelly Bus*

her baby brother
He's not even interesting. He doesn't know how to roll over. Or sit up. Or play Chinese checkers.
• from *Junie B. Jones and Her Big Fat Mouth*

the grocery store
I have rules at that place. Like no hollering the words I WANT ICE CREAM! And no calling Mother the name of big meanie when she won't buy it.
• from *Junie B. Jones and Some Sneaky Peeky Spying*

hamburger flippers
I runned all over with that thing. I flipped a rock and a flower and a dirt ball. Plus also, I flipped a dead lizard I found in the driveway. Then Mother took my flipper away.
• from *Junie B. Jones Has a Monster Under Her Bed*

clowns
Clowns are not normal people.
• from *Junie B. Jones and That Meanie Jim's Birthday*

grown-up words
Mother followed me. Her face looked suspicious. *Suspicious* is the grown-up word for *I think maybe you might be fibbing*.
• from *Junie B. Jones Is a Beauty Shop Guy*

acting like a lady
See how still I am sitting? I am not even squirming. On account of grown-up ladies do not get ants in their pants, that's why.
• from *Junie B. Jones Is (Almost) a Flower Girl*

quality entertainment
After that, Room Nine clapped and whistled and hooted and hollered. 'Cause who doesn't love chain-saw jugglers? That's what I would like to know!
• from *Junie B. Jones and the Mushy Gushy Valentime*

Barbara Park says:

66 When I tell people that I grew up in New Jersey, they're usually surprised to learn that my small hometown was surrounded by farms. And believe it or not, just like Junie B. Jones, I visited a farm on my very first field trip.

I still remember the thrill of getting off the bus and seeing all the cows and pigs up close and personal. But the best part of the trip was getting to see the baby animals. I couldn't imagine how wonderful it would be to live with all those little 'pets' right in your own backyard.

I was shocked that Junie B. wasn't as excited about her farm visit as I was about mine. But then again, the thought of a mean old rooster with peckery lips might have made me want to stay on the bus, too. And I never even considered the scary ponies... 99